A Note to Parents and Caregivers:

Read-it! Readers are for children who are just starting on the amazing road to reading. These beautiful books support both the acquisition of reading skills and the love of books. In some books, there are common sounds at the beginning, the ending, or even in the middle of many familiar words. It is good preparation for reading to help students listen for and repeat these sounds as part of having fun with words.

The RED LEVEL presents familiar topics using common words and repeating sentence patterns.

The BLUE LEVEL presents new ideas using a larger vocabulary and varied sentence structure.

The YELLOW LEVEL presents more challenging ideas, a broad vocabulary, and wide variety in sentence structure.

The GREEN LEVEL presents more complex ideas, an extended vocabulary range, and expanded language structures.

When sharing a book with your child, read in short stretches, pausing often to talk about the pictures. Have your child turn the pages and point to the pictures and familiar words. And be sure to reread favorite stories or parts of stories.

There is no right or wrong way to share books with children. Find time to read with your child, and pass on the legacy of literacy.

Adria F. Klein, Ph.D.
Professor Emeritus
California State University
San Bernardino, California

Managing Editors: Bob Temple, Catherine Neitge
Creative Director: Terri Foley
Editors: Jerry Ruff, Patricia Stockland
Editorial Adviser: Mary Lindeen
Designer: Amy Bailey Muehlenhardt
Storyboard development: Charlene DeLage
Page production: Picture Window Books
The illustrations in this book were prepared digitally.

Picture Window Books
5115 Excelsior Boulevard
Suite 232
Minneapolis, MN 55416
877-845-8392
www.picturewindowbooks.com

Printed in the United States of America.

Library of Congress Cataloging-in-Publication Data
Blackaby, Susan.
Hatching chicks / by Susan Blackaby ; illustrated by Amy Bailey Muehlenhardt.
p. cm. — (Read-it! readers classroom tales)
Summary: Mrs. Shay brings to class seven eggs from her hen, and her students take care of them until they hatch.
ISBN 1-4048-0585-0 (hardcover)
[1. Eggs—Fiction. 2. Chickens—Fiction. 3. Schools—Fiction.] I. Muehlenhardt, Amy Bailey, 1974- ill. II. Title. III. Series.
PZ7.B5318Hat 2004
[E]—dc22 2004007390

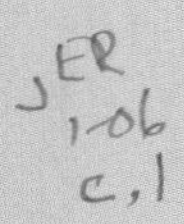

Hatching Chicks

By Susan Blackaby

Illustrated by Amy Bailey Muehlenhardt

Special thanks to our advisers for their expertise:

Adria F. Klein, Ph.D.
Professor Emeritus, California State University
San Bernardino, California

Susan Kesselring, M.A.
Literacy Educator
Rosemount-Apple Valley-Eagan (Minnesota) School District

PICTURE WINDOW BOOKS
Minneapolis, Minnesota

Mrs. Shay came into class.
She held up a picture of a hen.

“This is Betty. She has a nest in my shed. Thanks to Betty, I have lots of eggs,” said Mrs. Shay.

"Chicks come from eggs. We can hatch eggs in class. We will not use a nest. We will use this box."

Mrs. Shay set seven eggs in the box. "This box is made to hatch eggs," she said.

The box had lights to keep the eggs warm.
"If the eggs get cold, the chicks will not hatch," said Mrs. Shay.

The box had water in the pan to keep the eggs wet.

"If the eggs get too dry, the chicks will not hatch," said Mrs. Shay.

"How long will it take for the chicks to hatch?" asked Kat.

"Three weeks," said Mrs. Shay.

“Jess will check the eggs each day. Jess will help us keep track of our chicks.”

Mrs. Shay showed the kids how to turn the eggs.

"If the eggs sit still, the chicks will not hatch."

The kids helped Jess. They turned the eggs three times a day.

A week went by.

MARCH						
						1
2	3	4	5	6	7	8
9	10	11	12	13	14	15
16	17	18	19	20	21	22
23/30	24/31	25	26	27	28	29

"We can see the chicks inside the shell," said Mrs. Shay.

Mrs. Shay pulled the shades.
Then she held up an egg.
She aimed a light at the shell.

"Look for a dark spot in the egg. The dark spot is a chick," said Mrs. Shay.

The kids helped Jess. They checked the eggs. Every egg had a chick inside.

A week went by.

“Why does hatching take so long?” asked Bob.

“The chick starts out the size of a speck,” said Mrs. Shay.

“It grows inside the shell. Then the chick gets big. It uses its egg tooth to crack the shell.”

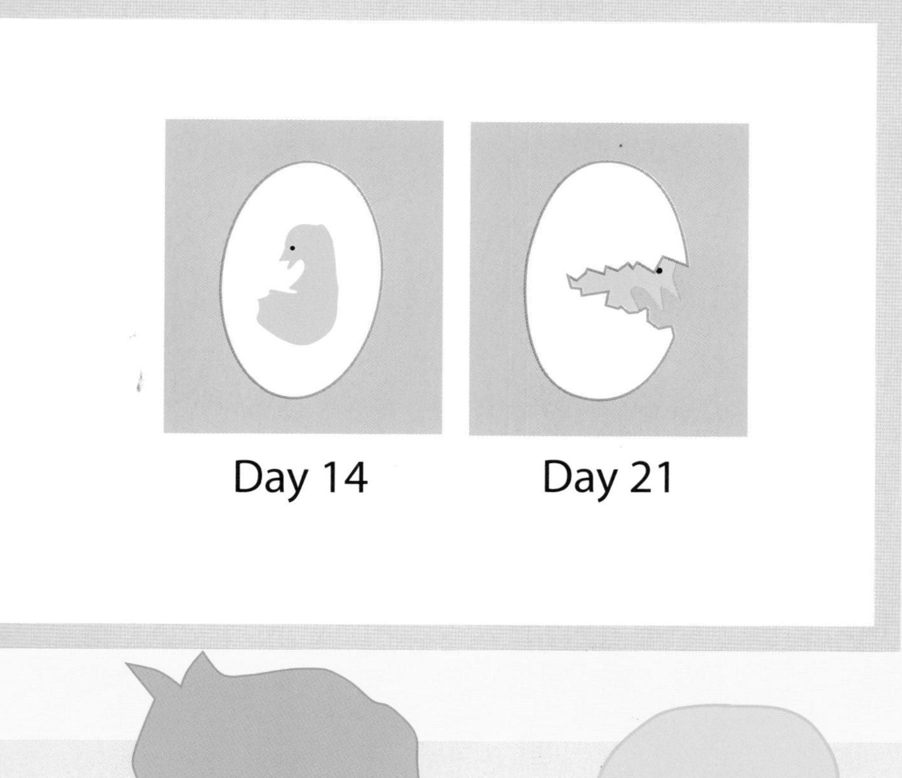

A week went by.

“Hatching takes too long,”

said Bob.

"Be glad you are not a hen," said Mrs. Shay. "At home, Betty sits on her nest until the eggs hatch. You get to run and play while you wait."

The kids went out to play.

They threw the ball in the net.

They went on the swings.

Then Mrs. Shay called them to go inside.

“Time to work,” said Mrs. Shay.
“Sit quietly at your desks.
I do not want to hear a peep.”
The kids took out their red pencils.

Peep! Peep!

"I hear a peep!" said Sunny.

"It came from the box," said Kat.

Jess jumped up. He checked the eggs. He saw a crack. “They are hatching!” said Jess.

One, two, three, four, five, six,
seven chicks hatched.

The next day, the kids held the fluffy yellow chicks.

"These chicks are the best," said Jess.

One week went by. Then seven yellow chicks went home to live in Mrs. Shay's shed.

Levels for *Read-it!* Readers

Read-it! Readers help children practice early reading skills with brightly illustrated stories.

Red Level: Familiar topics with frequently used words and repeating patterns.

I Am in Charge of Me by Dana Meachen Rau
Let's Share by Dana Meachen Rau

Blue Level: New ideas with a larger vocabulary and a variety of language structures.

At the Beach by Patricia M. Stockland
The Playground Snake by Brian Moses
The Word of the Day by Susan Blackaby

Yellow Level: Challenging ideas with an expanded vocabulary and a wide variety of sentences.

A Fire Drill with Mr. Dill by Susan Blackaby
Hatching Chicks by Susan Blackaby
Marvin, the Blue Pig by Karen Wallace
Moo! by Penny Dolan
Pippin's Big Jump by Hilary Robinson
A Pup Shows Up by Susan Blackaby
The Queen's Dragon by Anne Cassidy
Tired of Waiting by Dana Meachen Rau

Green Level: More complex ideas with an extended vocabulary range and expanded language structures.

Classroom Cookout by Susan Blackaby
Clever Cat by Karen Wallace
Flora McQuack by Penny Dolan
Izzie's Idea by Jillian Powell
Naughty Nancy by Anne Cassidy
The Roly-Poly Rice Ball by Penny Dolan
Sausages! by Anne Adeney
Sunny Bumps the Drum by Susan Blackaby
The Truth About Hansel and Gretel by Karina Law

A complete list of _Read-it!_ Readers is available on our Web site: www.picturewindowbooks.com